Rip's Secret Spot

Rip's Secret Spot

Kristi T. Butler

Illustrated by Joe Cepeda

Green Light Readers
Harcourt, Inc.
San Diego   New York   London

www.harcourt.com

First Green Light Readers edition 2000
Green Light Readers is a registered trademark of Harcourt, Inc.

Library of Congress Cataloging-in-Publication Data
Butler, Kristi T.
Rip's secret spot/Kristi T. Butler; illustrated by Joe Cepeda.
—1st Green Light Readers ed.
p. cm.
"Green Light Readers."
Summary: When Pat, Mom, and Dad mysteriously lose some of their things, the
family dog helps find them.
[1. Dogs—Fiction. 2. Lost and found possessions—Fiction.]
I. Cepeda, Joe, ill. II. Title.
PZ7. B97735Ri 2000
[E]—dc21 99-50802
ISBN 0-15-202640-1
ISBN 0-15-202646-0 (pb)

C E G H F D B
C E G H F D B (pb)

Pat could not find her frog.

"Who has my frog?"

Mom could not find her pin.
"Who has my pin?"

Dad could not find his hat.
"Who has my hat?"

Pat, Mom, and Dad looked
for the missing things.

"Pat," called Dad, "look at Rip.
He ran off fast."

"Rip is sniffing the grass.
Now he is digging."

"That dog digs all the time," said Pat.

"My hat is in that hole," said Dad.
"There is my frog!" shouted Pat.

"All our things are there!
My pin is there, too," said Mom.

"I think that's Rip's secret spot!"
said Dad.

"Let's dig up our things," said Pat.
"We will put *this* in the hole for Rip!"

Meet the Illustrator

Joe Cepeda reads a story many times before he works on the pictures for it. He doesn't start drawing until he knows the story well. First he draws the place where the story happens. He draws the people last. He likes to make the characters look like people he really knows!